OVER THESE COBBLESTONES

An Álamos Sojourn

EMILY PREECE

Copyright © 2009, Emily Preece by All rights reserved.

Most Trafford titles are also available at major online book retailers.

Note for Librarians: A cataloguing record for this book is available from Library and Archives Canada at www.collectionscanada.ca/amicus/index-e.html

Printed in Victoria, BC, Canada.

ISBN: 978-1-4269-2207 (sc)

We at Trafford believe that it is the responsibility of us all, as both individuals and corporations, to make choices that are environmentally and socially sound. You, in turn, are supporting this responsible conduct each time you purchase a Trafford book, or make use of our publishing services. To find out how you are helping, please visit www.trafford.com/responsiblepublishing.html

Our mission is to efficiently provide the world's finest, most comprehensive book publishing service, enabling every author to experience success. To find out how to publish your book, your way, and have it available worldwide, visit us online at www.trafford.com

Trafford rev. 6/23/2009

 www.trafford.com

North America & international
toll-free: 1 888 232 4444 (USA & Canada)
phone: 250 383 6864 ♦ fax: 250 383 6804 ♦ email: info@trafford.com

The United Kingdom & Europe
phone: +44 (0)1865 487 395 ♦ local rate: 0845 230 9601
facsimile: +44 (0)1865 481 507 ♦ email: info.uk@trafford.com

10 9 8 7 6 5 4 3 2 1

Contents

Dedicated to those who have moved on
from places such as this
to live their different lives.
May they remember their past.
May visitors to Álamos know the present

"....Just to live in Álamos is a full-time job; you don't have to 'do' anything. The idle pursuit of making a living is pushed to one side, where it belongs, in favor of living itself, a task of such immediacy, variety, beauty, and excitement that one is powerless to resist its wild embrace."

Quotation from E.B. White, with "Álamos" substituted for White's New England.

Kathryn Pabst Rodriguez
Álamos, Sonora

Map of Sonora, Mexico

INTRODUCTION

THIS place I lovingly write about is Álamos, a small town of about 10,000 inhabitants in the northern Mexico state of Sonora. It is situated some five hundred miles south of the Arizona-Mexico border past Magdalena, Hermosillo, San Carlos-Guaymas, and Ciudad Obregón to Navojoa. Here one turns inland toward rising terrain, traversing a 'spur' road that dead-ends at Álamos.

The distinctive features of this town are its people, and its colonial architecture, reminiscent of the Iberean influence of more than two hundred and fifty years ago, when architects from Spain laid out the town's blueprint. Block-sized family compounds with shaded portals encompassed the central church and plaza, and outward radiating cobblestone streets provided the network for traffic. Today, by city ordinance, new construction in Álamos must resemble the old; and the colonial look of the town makes us think we've taken a walk back through time to get here. The people are friendly, the children adorable, and it is said the young ladies of Álamos are some of the most beautiful in all of Mexico.

My best friend and husband, Bill, introduced me to Álamos over a quarter century ago. It was here that we were married, and it was here that we escaped for brief respites during all those years operating a busy aviation venture in Scottsdale, Arizona. Now retired, Álamos has become our second home, and we are comfortable here. Life, death, and politics go on in this place as in any other part of the country, or the world, for that matter.

I have written this book as a memoir to share descriptively the pleasures and peculiarities of Mexican small town life at the turn of the twenty-first century. It is hoped that by vicariously spending a week in this Sonoran colonial pueblo, the reader may observe ordinary days, interact with the people, and take part in the celebrations and rituals of Mexican life as they occur over these cobblestones of Álamos.

Emily Preece / <ins>alamosartist@aol.com</ins>

Álamos, Mexico

May, 2009

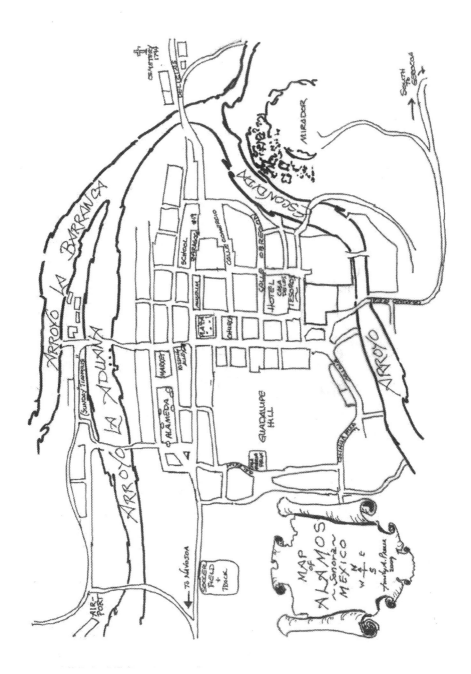

PROLOGUE

A string of Spanish colonial pueblos is tucked in alongside the backbone of the Mexican Sierra Madre mountain range in what was once the kingdom of New Spain. They are evidence that the Spanish discovered rich ore deposits in those areas in the 17th and 18th Centuries, and harvested them to the "greater honor and glory of God and country". The *Camino Real* (Kings Road) was built to connect these mining towns for delivery of gold and silver from the northern-most mines in Álamos, Sonora, south to what is today Mexico City. Returning mule-trains brought the latest news, equipment, and other purchases as dictated by the wealth and whims of the rich mine owners. From north to south, the mining towns along the route included Álamos in the state of Sonora, Fresnillo in Zacatecas, Real de Bolano in Jalisco, Ciudad de Zacatecas in Zacatecas, Real de Catorce in San Luis Potosi, Chico and Real de Monte in Hidalgo, Tlalpujahua in Michoacan, Real de Oro in México, Taxco in Guerrero, and Guanajuato.

The "golden age" for these mining centers ended when extraction costs exceeded end-product results, which was accelerated by a lack of capital, infighting for property rights, indigenous attacks, and cholera. By the early 1900's, only the most vibrant of the colonial mining towns had diversified their occupations and work force to insure sufficient growth, becoming the thriving metropolises they are today. Guanajuato and Zacatecas are two good examples. The cities that didn't make it through this period floundered and languished. Those residents who were young and able left the area to make their livelihood elsewhere, leaving behind virtual ghost towns.

The pueblo of Álamos suffered this latter fate, made worse when more modern transportation in Mexico demanded a better system of roadways and what is now Highway 15 was laid out. It originated at Sonora's northern most border town of Nogales, and from there headed south. This new road would not pass through Álamos, which lay nestled in southern Sonora between the base of the Sierra Madre Occidental and a few stand-alone mountains to the west. The town would be by-passed. For many years thereafter a rough, rocky road from the town of Navojoa would be the only real connection Álamos would have with the mainstream world.

In this now seemingly cloistered condition, the block-sized family compounds designed by Spanish architects in the 1750's to house wealthy Spanish mine owners and their extended families were divided up or abandoned. Mother Nature reclaimed what was originally hers, and many interiors deteriorated beyond repair. A once thriving community of many thousands dwindled to only a few hundred; the economic basis shifted down – way down. Álamos became known as *Álamos casas caidas* (falling houses Álamos).

Ranching and farming out in the surrounding Sonoran desert landscape seemed to hold together what was left of the community, until the late 1950s, when foreigners found and took an interest in this off-the-beaten-track colonial ruin as a reprieve from their hectic *Norte Americano* lifestyle.

Somewhat revitalized by the influx of *extranjeros* and their money during the 1950's, 1960's and beyond, Álamos experienced a rebirth. Reconstructions started, time healed the wounds of insurrection and upheaval, and the city was elevated to her rightful place among other Spanish Colonial treasures, first by being recognized by Mexico as a National Colonial Monument, and more recently being named a *Pueblo Mágico* by Mexico's Secretary of Tourism.

Today, as we enter the twenty first Century, about two hundred and fifty non-Mexican households are interspersed among the forty-some *barrios*, or neighborhoods, of Álamos. New construction in and around the city closely duplicates the ambiance of older, or restored buildings. As of this writing, work is underway to enhance the colonial appearance of the original *Centro* area by rerouting electric services underground. The city is striving to gain status as a UNESCO World Heritage site. A new multi-lane highway connects Álamos to Navojoa and the major north- south-bound traffic on Highway 15, and a new, paved road soon will link Álamos to Masiaca, a village to the south.

Ironically, too, Álamos has come full-circle and mining has once again started to the north and south of town, where modern methods and machinery are removing copper, gold and silver from the surrounding hillsides. What will be recorded in the history books about this deja vu encounter with the past is yet to be seen.

But this is not a history book. Plenty of those (see Books and Websites Referred to and Recommended)) already exist for your reading pleasure. So, this is where history stops, and the *historias* begin.

My husband and I first visited Álamos in the early 1980's. We were married here, and shortly thereafter purchased a home located within one of the original central blocks of town. The anecdotes you will read here are the real events I have witnessed, with additional details supplied by trustworthy residents of Álamos. These stories and the feelings I hope they invoke have come from my journals, and are recorded here to be passed on as "snapshots" of life in a small Mexican colonial town at the dawn of the twenty first Century.

Spanish words when first used are italicized, with English translations in parenthesis where necessary.

The author's home at Calle Comerico 19.

CHAPTER 1

Sunday

It's an early Sunday morning in March. The sun has risen on a beautiful, cool, blue-sky day, although our latitude dictates that we'll be in for high temperatures as the hours wear on, even this early in spring. With that in mind, I decide to take advantage of the pleasant morning conditions to do a little pruning on the two cedar trees that grow on either side of the stairway approach to our historic, colonial-style home, at *Calle Comercio 19*, one block off the main plaza of the town. The rise from the cobblestone street below to entry level is about four feet. A wrought-iron fence with a gate surrounds the landing in front of the house, and the two small trees planted at street-level have grown taller than the railing around the fence. I figure the trimming should only take a few minutes of my time, but would still rather do it while it is cooler outside. Armed with garden gloves and pruning shears, I step outside and start snipping.

After a few moments I look up to see riding down our wide, cobbled street a man on his bicycle. His young son accompanies him, perched side-saddle across the bar of the bike. As they pass, the young father simply says *"Hoy es día de descanso, no de trabajo"* (Today is a day of rest, not of work), and peddles on. I turn, smile weakly, and reply, more to myself than to him, that I'm only doing a little work – "*no mucho*", and as he disappears up the street toward the church and the plaza I finish up quickly. Discarding my clippings, I go back inside and almost sheepishly return the gloves and shears to their resting place in the storage shed. Out of respect for the "day of rest" and the people of Álamos, any further gardening will have to wait for a week day.

The church bells are beginning to ring for the second Sunday Catholic mass. We had been awakened earlier this morning by the rousing chimes signaling the first service of the day at 6:30 am. The notification process for each mass at the church on the plaza, *Nuestra Señora de la Purisma Concepcíon* (Our Lady of the Immaculate Conception), dates back to life before wrist-watches, and is a three-fold process. First bells are rung one-half hour before the worship begins, followed by a second-call at fifteen minutes prior to the appointed time. Each successive carillon seems a bit more prolonged and clamorous than the previous one. Finally, as the celebrant priest and altar boys make their entrance from the sacristy out to the altar and mass begins, the bells are rung with abandon one final time. One had better be in a pew by then.

The 8:30 a.m. convocation is the children's service. Young school children are expected to attend and sit up front on either side of the main aisle – boys to the left, and girls to the right. Adult "monitors" cruise either side of the rows of pews to quickly squelch any fidgeting or antics. Kids will be kids in any country, I guess. The priest's sermon is directed toward the youngsters and always carries a lesson geared to their level of understanding. Things wrap up quickly after communion, and with a few necessary announcements and a final blessing, the mass ends. A pressing crowd of parishioners streams out the doors – the children practically running – and then everyone disperses. Most of the crowd heads across the plaza and down the narrow, cobbled, *callejón de beso*, Álamos's famous Kissing Alley, on foot. They are on their way to the commercial shopping area and the Sunday, open-air *tianguis* (open air bazaar-type market), which lines the banks of the usually dry arroyo which splits the town into two halves. This festive *tianguis* draws vendors from neighboring areas, as well as shoppers from the outlying ranches who come into Álamos for their weekly purchases. I need to shop as well, and fall in behind the church goers.

On Sundays, a policeman directs pedestrians and vehicular traffic at the far corner of the market. Today people have the right-of-way, and the cars and trucks must wait their turn. A *paleta* (ice-cream and frozen juice bar) cart waits for hungry shoppers on the other side of the crossing, the vendor nonchalantly jingling the bar of bells along the handle while waiting for his next customer. Soon, a small boy is reaching past the square opening of the small, square cart into the coolness of the dark interior to make his selection. His mother holds him practically upside-down as he struggles to grasp his prize. Finally, the youngster gives up, and his mother has to get it for him. I pass on.

Farther ahead, the smooth paving stones end, and the way across the dry river bottom narrows. Approaching the first stands of the Sunday-only open air bazaar market, I must maneuver sideways through rows of fresh vegetables and shoes on the right, clothing and second-hand kitchen gadgets on the left, and cross the riverbed to the other side. It's hard to walk past the tempting chocolate and *tres leches* (three milks) cakes for sale by the slice. A very generous piece sells for ten pesos, or about a dollar. Even if one has resisted that temptation, there will be more opportunities to test resolve. I turn left and start meandering past the stands offering fruits, vegetables, clothing, shoes, CD's, DVD's, used appliances, household goods, a key making service, tools and potted flowers and plants. Shopping is already brisk. Some of the earlier church goers are still making purchases or eating. Trucks that have come in from the outlying ranchos line the arroyo, and are being filled with a week's worth of food and necessities that will be shared by all residents there.

A street vendor gourmand's feast awaits those who can no longer resist temptation. Today, in addition to the regular fruit cups with *pica de gallo* (nip of the rooster) sauce, fresh, ripe mangos are being sold as an eat-it-now snack. For fifteen or twenty pesos one gets a ripe, peeled mango, presented on a stick, cut decoratively to resemble an open flower and sprinkled with hot chili sauce and a squeeze of lemon juice. Further along, I can smell the *chicharones*, crispy pieces of deep-fried pig's skin, being cooked and sold by weight along with fresh chicken and eggs. At the far end of the market the aroma of hot fish tacos call to the senses, and beautiful baskets of ripe strawberries, served with cream, sit neatly in rows warming in the sun, waiting to be purchased. More *chicharones* at the very end – just in case you missed them further back. Dogs lounge patiently, waiting for someone to drop a bite or throw them a scrap.

All the while, oom-pa-pa *ranchero* music blares from the stand of a CD vendor who is competing for sales with another vendor farther down – his music ALSO blaring. DVD movies including popular children's films and recent releases are available, at a very affordable two for fifty pesos. A mother passes in the opposite direction with one youngster in tow and another, swaddled in a colorful *reboso* (shawl), at her breast. Foot-traffic only in this market area. Conversation, hugs, and handshakes everywhere. A chance to see and greet many whose faces I know, but whose names I've not yet learned in all these years here.

It's time to leave. Smiles all around. Friendship, a few purchases, and just enough change left to buy a cup of fresh fruit – crisp jicama, crunchy coconut, watermelon, orange and pineapple– with a generous squeeze of lemon juice, before I start a leisurely walk back home. I decide to exit at this far end of the *tianguis* with my shopping items, rather than retrace my steps through the now quite crowded venue.

The stalls dead-end at another river-bed crossing, and just beyond is the gated entryway to the backyard of a private residence. The gate is open, and my eye is drawn to a portable canopy with the *Tecate* beer logo on it. Beyond the canopy, beautiful flower arrangements decorate the elevated back portal of the residence. Closer observation reveals that a *velorio* (wake) is in progress. The flowers flank a brown, lacquered coffin lying in state for viewing prior to the final mass and burial later in the day. Market traffic streams by as family and friends solemnly come and go from the house. The men congregate near the gate to visit while the women take seats under the *Tecate* canopy to get out of the sun. New arrivals enter the compound and pay their respects to the immediate family members, who are up on the porch near the remains of the loved one – soul already departed – before falling back to join the other visitors for a chat. A funeral hearse is parked near-by in the arroyo awaiting the appointed hour for the drive to the church for mass and then out to the *Panteón* for burial. In the midst of the bustling *tianguis* traffic, life – and death – move on.

Most everyone's Sundays here are devoted to family and friends, conversation and relaxation. As the day progresses, the center of activity will shift from the *tianguis* back to the plaza in front of the church. Already the regular weekend vendors are at the park-like square, setting up their stands, which will provide more opportunities later today to sample tacos, corn-on-the-cob, hot and cold drinks, cakes, candies and deep fried pastry rolled in sugar called *churros*. When the final chorus of church bells rings for the 6:00 p.m. mass, it will be well attended, because for many it's a prelude to evening activities and socializing around the plaza.

At about 7:00 p.m., Bill and I decide to take our black labrador, Gina, out for a twilight walk in front of our home on Calle Comercio. Gina is fourteen years old, so usually only goes as far as she needs to do her "business", and then is ready to return to the house and the comfort of the living-room couch. This evening, however, is different. Something undetectable to us becomes blatantly evident to Gina's acute sense of smell, and in her mind, whatever it is <u>must</u> be investigated! Out the front door, and down the steps, Gina turns right and immediately starts walking with purpose, actually pulling hard on the leash that Bill is holding. Up Calle Comercio, bearing right onto Calle Zaragosa, past the Bartholomew Salido grade-school and Pollo's Restaurant and still farther on, to the plaza. Then, without hesitation, she turns left and leads us directly to Fortino's taco stand, where she sits down and looks up at us. Gina has taken us out for dinner! Bill and I look at each other and laugh as we sit down at Fortino's clean, white picnic tables, draped with colorful tablecloths and set with bowls containing all the extra toppings to accompany beef tacos. Bill orders for all three of us: "*Tres y dos y dos de maiz*"... (three corn-tortilla beef tacos for Bill, two for me, and two for Gina, of course!). The seating is family-style, with

Mexicans and *gringos*, sharing the same condiments and lively conversation while dining. With a friendly *buen provecho* (good appetite) to those who have joined us while we were eating, we rise from the table to give our seats to waiting customers, pay our tab, and leave.

Before retracing our steps back to the house, we join everyone else for one leisurely stroll around the plaza. Darkness has fallen, and the evening breezes stir the fronds of the tall palm trees planted around the elevated kiosk placed on this public square over a century ago. Wrought iron fencing and benches surround the plaza walkways; and the protected garden areas are blooming with roses, hibiscus and bougainvillea. Three of the four streets around this park-like square just in front of the church are closed off to vehicular traffic on Sundays, offering ample space for families young and old to gather and meet friends, children to scamper about, and teenagers to mingle with their peers. Mom and pop vendors offer sweets, drinks, and snacks. Juke-box and guitar music is heard from a corner kids hang-out, across the street. Stereo music resounds from the cars allowed passage on the open side of the square. We slowly make our way around the plaza, adding our presence to all this activity, and enjoying the vibrancy of the Sunday evening social life of Álamos.

In preparation for the beginning of another work week, all this liveliness eventually winds down, and one by one the vendors remove their stands from around the plaza and truck them away. By early Monday morning, the evidence of Sunday's festivities will be gone, and only the lonely street sweeper wielding his twig broom in the colorful debris will know just how much fun everyone had.

Mother dog gingerly carries by its knot, a plump, blue plastic bag about the size of a basketball.

CHAPTER 2

Monday

After a restful night's sleep, Álamos resumes its week-day heart beat with the arrival of the first rays of light on Monday morning. We hear it in the sounds of braying, barking, and crowing that help to awaken the town, while early workers softly pad their way over the cobblestones in front of the house. Mothers walk their youngsters, dressed in crisp school uniforms and carrying little back-packs, to the grade school just up the street. As the children gather in the inner courtyard of the school to start their day of learning, their happy, playful chatter wafts from the school-yard over several residential walls into our patio. Soon, the brash 'clang-clang-clang' of a singular school bell announces the appointed hour for lessons to begin. After announcements by the principal and the conducting of group exercises over the school's loud speaker, the children shuffle off to their class rooms, and our courtyard becomes quiet once again, except for the pleasing sound of the trickling fountain and a lone *paloma* cooing up in the *cedra* tree.

Prior to starting my *que haceres* (household "to-do" list) for the day, I step outside to inhale the fresh morning air and feel the warmth of the sun. The pace of life in Álamos always allows time for a brief chat with any friends or neighbors one might meet, and my first encounter this morning is with fellow American and Calle Comercio neighbor, Peter Combs.

As we stand out in the middle of the street talking about daily and world events, a mother dog and one of her pups go trotting past us in the direction of the church and the plaza. The mother appears to be a golden retriever-Shepard-'and-something-else' mix – a common breed found around Álamos, to be sure. Her young pup is jet black, short legged, and has to do at least double-time to keep up with the mother. And so Peter and I chat, and they pass by. We are still conversing some minutes later when mother dog and her puppy reappear, returning from their mission, which was apparently to find some breakfast. Mother dog gingerly carries, by its knot, a plump, tightly tied blue plastic bag about the size of a basket ball, obviously someone's garbage that had been discarded further up the street. The proud new owner and her offspring are walking with real purpose now, headed for home turf, or some other safe haven where the mother can open and investigate her booty, hopefully providing for herself and her young one. The pup scurries along one side, behind, then along the other side, breathless with just trying to keep up, and most anxious with anticipation to see what mom has procured for them both. It is a humorous but loving scene, proving the adage that one man's trash is, indeed, treasure for another. Peter and I chuckle, bid farewell, and go our separate ways.

With the start of any new week comes the responsibility for certain things that must be accomplished. Doing laundry certainly comes to mind as one of those chores that never really goes away. Some here have the luxury of owning a washing machine; but most residents of Álamos still use an outdoor wash station built from adobe bricks and cement. Clothing washed by hand or by machine both require the essential ingredient of water, and that element has been an issue in this municipality for many years.

Our precious little enclave lies in a unique area of southern Sonora, best described as a 'dry tropical forest'. Water is a cherished and respected commodity. No lakes, rivers, or streams feed the town directly; instead, a watershed from the *Sierra Madre de Álamos* mountains feeds the water table and water is pumped out and up to a city storage and distribution system with an antiquated infrastructure that allows as much to seep out as it delivers. Innovative use of *hule* (inner-tube rubber pieces) repairs those *fugas* (leaks) that ooze enough to become apparent at street level. It is more economical to simply control the hours and days of city water delivery, than to tear up and re-do the entire municipal water system. And so water is rationed.

Álamos residents have become accustomed to water rationing. There is no published schedule to the supply. For most residents, whatever day you turn on the faucet and have water is the day you can take advantage of it and use it. Many of the larger properties have a *pozo* (well) with a *pila* (below ground storage tank) to store water, giving them ready access to it at any time. Others may store water reserves in an elevated, gravity-fed water holding tank called a *tinaca*. Potable bottled water is sold door-to-door. Only recently have residential water meters been installed throughout town, and a new billing system based on individual usage has been initiated. Not really expensive, an average month's bill for water, sewer and garbage pick-up services averages about fifty pesos per month. Even so, wasting water is not tolerated. A *chorro* (stream) of water running out from a private property into the public streets is reported and followed up on by the OOMAPAS (Álamos municipal water company). It might result in the removal of one's meter and a subsequent *multa* (fine) that must be paid for the service to be restored.

In simpler households many times, the laundry rinse water gets recycled to become wash water, and the well-used wash water is channeled or carried away to nourish a few sparse seedlings or trees in the yard. Flowers and blooms are coaxed and raised like small children to grow and prosper, and a yard featuring any kind of colorful botanical display is to be admired not only for its simple beauty, but with the knowledge of how lovingly and painstakingly each plant was nurtured.

Washing is line-dried or simply draped over fences. I, like most *gringos*, have the luxury (and expense.) of an electric dryer. Unlike water, electricity is very expensive here, and the bi-monthly bills for our household reflect the usage of many creature comforts. In addition to the aforementioned dryer, our family enjoys the things that most families north of the border come to expect: lights, a TV, microwave oven, coffee pot, computer, vacuum, and the list goes on. It is not unusual for an average electric bill at our house to run 3,000 or 4,000 pesos per (two-month) billing cycle when all the modern electric conveniences are used at will. A more conservative Mexican household can expect a typical bill of two hundred and fifty to four hundred pesos for a two-month period. Burning a single lightbulb is the most economical route, and even this produces a bill that may be hard to pay for those on a limited income. And that brings me to the story of Don Martín Leyva.

On Calle Galeana where the street widens prior to dividing, is the childhood home of Mexican film actress Maria Felix (1914-2002). Just across the wide street, between two colonial-style homes at street level, is a sliver of an entrance made of compacted dirt, only wide enough for one person to pass through and back into the small confines of a very humble abode. It would be easy to miss this entrance if you didn't know it was there. I had passed by it numerous times and never noticed the entry. Today, as well, I probably would not have noticed, had someone not called out to me softly as I was walking on the way to a friend's house further up the street. Pulled back from somewhere deep in my own thoughts, I realized it was an elderly gentleman sitting outside his doorway on an upturned five-gallon bucket who had called out. I went over to respond to Don Martín's greeting.

Once I got closer to him and he could see me better, he said, "Oh, *Señora*, I'm sorry. I thought you were *'Tericita'* (Teri Shannon is proprietress of the "Red Door" B&B just up the street.)

"No", I replied, "I'm not *Tericita*, but may I help you?"

"I have this", he said, and showed me the curled-up electric bill in his hand. I looked at it. The charges were fifty eight pesos for the most recent two-month period – amounting to probably just a single bare light bulb sparingly used somewhere in the inner sanctum of his living area back in off the street.

"Perhaps you might help me with this bill.", he proposed. "I have nothing. I have nothing." he repeated.

I immediately opened my purse and pulled out a one hundred peso note, and gave it to him. It was only about ten dollars, but would more than cover the electric bill and leave some extra money for whatever extra little purchase he would choose to make.

"Muchas gracias, Señora", he said. *"Que Dios le bendiga"*, (that God will bless you).

Later, I learned from nearby residents that Don Martín Leyva comes from a good-sized family, but seems not to be helped much by any of his relatives. One neighbor prepares meals for the aged senior citizen, and others help with his bills. This neighborly assistance is typical in Álamos. On this day, the situation was just right that I would have the opportunity to meet this gentleman and help out, as well. As I returned from my sociable visit up the street, I could see Don Martín shuffling down Calle Galeana toward the Alameda, perhaps to go pay his electric bill.... and possibly have a beer with the change.

**Construction of above-ground vaults was common in the
Álamos cemetery many years ago**

CHAPTER 3

Tuesday

The relative nature by which Mexicans as a whole embrace death is a good lesson in reality. Without being showy or extravagant, morbid or macabre, everyone who passes on from this life into the next is given proper respect within the mandates of civil law, and the guidance of the Catholic Church.

Our very dear housekeeper, Lupe (Guadalupe Macias Escalante de Garcia), keeps on top of local news and happenings, most of which is still carried and spread from *barrio* to *barrio* by word of mouth. Upon her arrival on the days that she works, and after the ritual of morning greetings has taken place, she will usually share any neighborhood news with me. It usually goes something like this:

Lupe: "Do you know who has just died?"

Me: "No, who?"

Lupe: "Well, the mother of Techy, who works for the Jacobs household."

Me: "Oh. Really?"

Lupe: "Yes. Her mother was quite old, you know. Eighty-something...."

Me: "Ah, well, she had a good life, then."

Lupe: "Yes....."

There is a long pause. I can tell that Lupe still wants to say more. She continues:

Lupe: "I wonder if they will still have the wedding?"

Me: "The wedding? What wedding?"

Lupe: "Well, you know, Techy's daughter was to be married in a few weeks."

Me: "No, I didn't know that. Why wouldn't she still just get married?"

Lupe: "Oh, no, Emily. She can't have the church wedding and the reception. And the music. They couldn't have the music."

Me: "Oh, yes, I see. How long will they have to wait?"

Lupe: "Oh, *pues* (well), I would imagine three months, or so. I suppose they will just have the civil ceremony and then celebrate at some other time in the future."

Me: "Yes, I suppose so."

A death marks the beginning of a whirl-wind twenty-four hour period of activity for the immediate family of the departed. The *ataúd* (coffin) is purchased, and the body, without the benefit of embalming, is prepared for viewing before being brought back to the house. Things are pushed aside in the *portal* (outdoor covered living area) or *sala* (interior living room) to make room for the coffin, and anything available to sit on is placed near by. Word quickly spreads throughout the neighborhood of the impending period of visitation and vigil. An extensive support group of neighbors, friends, and family gather to pay their respects and pray during what will most likely be an over-night watch. Any out-of-town relatives able to traverse the distance and arrive within the period of mourning will do so, dropping everything and, if necessary, using the network of commercial busses that efficiently move the vast majority of the populace about the country. For extended families with members living *al otro lado* (north of the U.S./Mexican border), this visit may also serve as a family reunion of sorts where siblings, cousins, and in-laws can catch up on other family news.

Soon, flowers start arriving at the home, and the local florist shop is a flurry of activity preparing floral arrangements and attaching the sateen ribbon banners that identify the family, friend, or organization who wishes to be remembered to the survivors of the loved one. The banners usually are three-inches wide, and have the inscription written on them using glue from a squeeze bottle with a pointed tip attached. The ribbon is then inverted glue side down and pressed into a plate of loose glitter. Once picked up and shaken off, what remains is the raised and highlighted name with sparkle effects, with a crafty home-made quaintness that warms the heart.

The attentive vigil over the body continues into the next day until the hour for the Catholic mass of leave-taking approaches. The distinctive slow toll from the bell-tower echoes all over town as the coffin is transported to the church by whatever means is practical or affordable for the family, whether it be in the back of a pick-up truck, a station wagon, or by funeral hearse. At the church, with all the family members, friends and neighbors gathered around, able-bodied males carry the casket from street level up the well-worn wide granite staircase to the threshold of the church. The celebrant of the mass greets the procession at the door and after a prayer and blessing with holy water everyone follows the coffin inside and up the center aisle to a position of honor and respect in the nave.

Thus situated, friends and neighbors take turns as "attendants", standing along side the casket, the fingertips of one hand lightly touching its surface in a gesture of respect and fraternity to the family. Those wishing to take the place of someone in attendance simply walk up, tap the person on the shoulder, and step into their place. The person relieved steps aside and returns to the pew. This will go on all throughout the mass at intervals not dictated by anything other than the feelings of those present. It is a beautiful homage performed by friends and family members as a non-verbal statement that they will stand by their dearly departed friend and accompany them all the way through this life to the grave.

After mass, the procession forms to escort the remains of the loved one out to the *panteón*. The vehicle containing the casket will lead the procession, while family members follow slowly on foot, often reciting the rosary or a litany en route. In another great act of solidarity, the majority of the family's *barrio* neighbors will walk along with them. The cortege will wend it's way from the church down the cobblestones of Calle Comercio, across the arroyo, and bear right out Delicias road to the cemetery, a distance of about two kilometers. They may be followed by an open-bed truck carrying the floral arrangements and then by other vehicles of those mourners who choose not to walk out to the cemetery. Only occasionally will a mariachi band, accompany those in mourning, playing favorite tunes of the deceased. The semi-boisterous style of the musicians lifts the spirits of family and friends to some degree.

Preparations at the family burial plot have been ongoing since the news of the death... Although construction of stacked above-ground vaults, a la New Orleans, was customary in the Álamos cemetery many years ago, most burials are now in-ground. Once the opening has been dug, adobe bricks will line the vault-sized space that will receive the casket. This is completed before the procession arrives, and the workers respectfully will stand by while final prayers and blessings are bestowed by the priest. They then slowly lower the casket into the ground. A protective layer of adobe bricks is positioned on top while cement is hand-mixed on site and used to seal the adobe. Fill dirt and three huge cement plates are placed over the top and also sealed with a cement slurry. The flower arrangements are then mounded on and around the grave site in colorful contrast to the drabness of the surrounding dirt and wet cement. Any additional adornment is left to the family – plastering, granite headstones or statues – as can be afforded at some point in the future.

Slowly the funeral party members disburse and return home or to work. Some will continue to gather nightly at the home of the deceased for the next nine evenings, praying the rosary and providing additional comfort for grieving family members. If the one who has passed is a husband or matriarch of the family, his widow may go into *luto* (mourning) and choose to wear the traditional black or dark garb for the duration of the mourning period, anywhere from a year to the remainder of her life. Most families of the departed will adopt a subdued lifestyle for at least the next few months, putting off weddings, birthday parties, and other celebrations until they feel an acceptable period of time has passed out of respect for their loved one. So, it is no surprise when, one month later, shocked whispers circulate around town revealing that a young female relative of the deceased is seen dancing, yes, DANCING! ¡*Fíjate!* (can you imagine!?!) at a *quinceañera* , the traditional young girls' 15th birthday party. This brings the shadow of disgrace to the young lady's still-in-mourning family. In future generations the tradition of the period of *luto* may disintegrate. With that and other rituals gone, the basic foundation of close-knit family life as it still exists in Mexico may also erode. Only time will tell.

The Álamos cemetery is Álamos history. Realizing the amount of sentiments contained within it, the city recently refurbished and restored the oldest portions of the grounds and the boundary wall, enclosing the four-hectare area. A new lower-level has been opened and made available for burials, and public restrooms have been constructed on the premises.

Walkways among the oldest grave sites have been cobbled and restorative work and numbering/recording has been initiated in an effort to preserve and chronicle the earliest known grave sites. All the old family names are there: Urrea, Salido, Anaya, Almada, and Reyes, to name a few, which date from as far back as 1794. Most of the older grave markers now stand nameless. Time has eroded the dates and epitaphs from memory and from view. In addition to stacked, above-ground entombments, many elaborate chapel-like monuments, *capillas*, can be seen in this older section of the grounds, a testament to the wealth and family pride of past generations. The interesting thing about these shrines is that the *capillas* were constructed over an underground sepulcher where the caskets were interred. Behind the elaborate mausoleum, at ground level, a small wrought-iron door opens into a passageway only large enough for one man at a time to enter, and just wide enough for a casket to be passed through. Inside, several vaults are available to receive the remains, and then be sealed for eternity. The Reyes and Bartholomew Salido crypts are constructed in this manner. The elevated platform outside the Reyes chapel is large enough that it is often used as the site for celebration of mass during *Día de los Muertos* in November.

More than two hundred years of antiquity, conservatively eight to ten generations of life, struggles, conflicts, and love, are enclosed within the walls of the Álamos *panteon*. With all that emotion and spirit energy present, dare we not wonder if there might be *fantasmas* (ghosts) in the Álamos cemetery?

Patient wood-cutters simply waited for the crowns of intense color to appear, which was the *beso de la muerta* for the tree.

CHAPTER 4

Wednesday

The sweet scent of citrus blossoms hangs heavy in the still morning air, entering our screened bedroom windows to gently caress us awake. Our *cedra* tree is in full bloom, along with the *limón* and the kumquat or *naranjita*. Their waxy off-white blooms crowd every branch. This display will lure bees from far and wide to come and sample the heady juices; the buzzing sound is loud enough to make you think the hive itself is in the tree. Many drink so heartily that they fall to the ground in a stupor like drunken sailors. Spent blossoms and the *borracho* bees litter the courtyard like a light snowfall, creating a morning's work of sweeping for Lupe, when she arrives. A well-swept patio equates to a clean house in her mind, and this spring-time blooming ritual presents her with quite a challenge.

On this particular morning, however, we hear the distinctive chit-chit-chitter of hummingbirds darting among the blossoms. This is unusual. We rarely receive visits from groups of hummers during our winter months here; and certainly are not used to seeing many of them at one time, but today literally hundreds of them are sipping and hovering among the *cedra* tree blossoms. I wonder why so many of them have congregated here at our tree. A quick search on the computer leads me to a site dedicated to mapping the migrations of humming birds from their Central American winter locales to their summer dwellings in the United States and further north. The reports and input to date indicate that they are, indeed, on the move northbound, and their visit to our back yard fits right in with other recent sightings along their route. This, then, was a flock of migratory hummers making their way north, deciding to stop at our tree for breakfast before continuing on their journey. How nice of them to pick our patio as a stop along their way.

Enjoying fresh fruit from one's own orchard is a great joy. Ripened *cedra* resemble grapefruit in size and shape, with much thicker skins. When they ripen in fall, the pulp is not as juicy, and a bit more bland; a viable substitute for grapefruit at the breakfast table. The thick skins can be cut, trimmed, and candied for a treat reminiscent of the candied citrus peel used in making fruitcake.

Our other back yard citrus, the *limón* and *naranjita* trees, bloom at about the same time as the cedra, and produce abundantly as well. The *naranjita* fruit resembles a kumquat in size and shape and is rather curious in that the thin, easily peeled skin is actually edible, and tastes sweeter than the fruit itself. *Naranjitas* are often sold by street vendors in small plastic bags with chili powder generously sprinkled over them. The purchaser then kneads the bag to a homogeneous mash before making a small opening in the bottom of the bag and sucking out the paste. If this doesn't sound too appealing, you will like to hear that this fruit also makes a delicious marmalade. The recipe is very simple, and once cooked, is one of the few foodstuffs permitted across the border to give or enjoy anytime you want to remember the sweet yet tart taste of *naranjita*.

Mango trees also flourish in our area, and can bloom anytime from as early as November to as late as February. The blooming period stretches out over the period of a month or more. Not nearly as pleasing to the senses as the citrus, the clusters of tiny, uninteresting, scentless blossoms bloom prolifically, then die off and fall to litter the patio, making yet more work for Lupe. A few weeks later, pea-sized mangos start to appear where blossoms were successfully pollinated. The branches of the tree will begin to droop as the small fruits gain girth and weight. Occasional spring wind gusts force imperfect or non-developing thumb-sized mangos to fall, resounding like hail-stones off the neighbors corrugated metal portal roof. The hard green ovoid spheres continue to gain size and weight throughout the late spring and into summer while watchful eyes scan the branches awaiting the first changes in color indicating ripening fruits.

The experience of eating a sun-ripened mango right off the tree is something you will always remember. As the fruit matures, its color changes from green to yellow to a coral-orange with blush highlights. Not all mangos ripen at the same time. The wrought-iron *caracol* (snail-coil) staircase in our inner courtyard allows easy access to the flat roof, and puts us within arm's reach of many mangos. At mid-day or early afternoon, those that are ripe will be warm to the touch and feel almost life-like when picked. The skin will give some, and can be simply peeled off, revealing the fleshy, yellow-orange fibrous fruit. Just stand right there and slurp it in, peeling some more, working your way around the large flat seed. Some juice may run down your chin, but that's OK. This mango will taste better than any you may have ever purchased in a grocery store, and having patiently waited for almost five months makes it all the more pleasurable. The tree will continue to drop more ripened fruit than we can use for a month or more. Lupe will bag them up and place them in front of the house for passers-by to take. No food goes to waste in Mexico, and it is gratifying to share.

Another beautiful period of the year in the Sonoran desert area around Álamos is when the *amapa* trees are blooming. The dry, muted winter landscape creates a monochromatic palette for the explosion of brilliant pink and violet colors that mark the location of each of the sparsely located trees. A yellow blooming cousin to the pink *amapa* called the *"amapa amarilla"* can be occasionally seen along the Copper Canyon train route, but is more prolific further south in Mexico and down as far as Argentina. Long ago, the *amapas* were prized and harvested for their long, relatively straight trunks that are impervious to both moisture penetration and infestation by bugs and termites. Cut down, the harvested logs were used as weight-bearing roof beams, or *vigas maestras*, during colonial-era construction. Patient wood-cutters simply waited for the crowns of intense color to appear up in the hills, which was the *beso de la muerta* (kiss of death) for the tree, giving away its location and ending its life. It was not long before areas for miles around populated communities like Álamos became completely devoid of *amapa* trees.

The Mexican government initiated protection of the *amapa* trees in the mid-1900s. Some older homes in Álamos still have *vigas* of *amapa*, and some newer homes have *amapa* beams salvaged from antiquated ruins. When *amapa* could no longer be harvested for construction purposes, beams were fabricated from pine trees cut from the higher elevations in the neighboring Sierra Madre mountains. Not a viable substitute, the pine quickly twisted, split and rotted, and was ferociously eaten by termites.

Re-bar reinforced concrete beams, became the new material of choice from which *vigas* are still fabricated today. The concrete is poured into a wooden mold the same size of a pine *viga*, then, once released, painted brown to imitate the appearance of wood. They can look almost authentic, and are much more durable than any wood. Some *maestros* also are using steel beams faux-painted to give the effect of knotty sawn wood. A good artist can create quite believable effects.

Today, *amapa* can once again be seen blooming near populated areas. It is a particular treat to fly over the rising terrain surrounding Álamos while the *amapa* are at the height of their flowering. The effect is as if beautiful bouquets of lilacs or violets have been placed at random for miles around. Most stunning are the deep crevices and fingerling ravines to the east of Álamos toward the Copper Canyon. In these locals humans have never been able to disturb or harvest the trees, and the intense canopies of color are spectacular.

In addition to the beauty of the natural flora indigenous to this area and in the courtyards of many homes in Álamos, fresh-cut flowers adorn and impart sentiment to many memorable occasions as well. Our local florist, Antonio Gutierres Reyes, came from nearby Navojoa a few years ago to open a florist shop on the *Alameda*, first locating on the same side as the bus station, and later moving across the square into a newer vendor site in Doña Melba McGahey's building. Fresh flower deliveries to Antonio's shop usually arrive Tuesday and Friday afternoons, so I customarily make it a Wednesday morning errand to purchase fresh flowers for our kitchen and portal vases. Antonio offers tiger lilies, daisies, spider mums, carnations, bird-of-paradise, and gladiolas, accompanied by a wide selection of greenery, ferns, baby's breath, and long-stemmed roses. The shop is always cool inside, and the earthy smell of verdant shoots combines with the scents of the various flowers to produce a distinctive musky fragrance I associate with green houses and gardening.

I have enjoyed being the recipient of beautiful floral arrangements from Antonio's shop over the past few years on special occasions such as our anniversary, my birthday, and Valentines day, but the feeling I delight in the most is the walk home after my weekly purchase of freshly cut-flowers. My selection is always carefully wrapped and tied in a protective sleeve and handed to me like the bouquet awarded to Miss America. I pay what is owed and after an *Adiós*, emerge from the shop into the sunlight for my walk home with the flowers balanced in the crook of my left arm, carefully, like a newborn babe, but more like a prize for all to see.

For the four to five minute walk down the outside of the Mercado, up Kissing Alley, across the plaza, past Polo's Restaurant, and down Zaragosa to Calle Comercio, I am Miss America, or perhaps the *Reyna de Carnaval.* Everyone I pass looks, smiles, and nods approvingly as I pass with my flowers in arm. I, in turn, play my part to the fullest extent allowable – demeanor regal, posture erect, and gait flowing, knowing that the joy of having these flowers will last long after the walk home. Their color and beauty will enhance the portal or other chosen spots in our residence for the next week to come. Álamos, indeed is a place to appreciate Mother Nature's bounty of fruit and flowers.

**Block-sized family compounds with shaded portals
encompassed the central church and plaza.**

CHAPTER 5

Thursday

Most tourists who visit Álamos have nothing in common with those who keep Jimmy Buffet's *"Margaritaville"* a familiar lyric. Fun-seeking party animals slathered with suntan lotion who bake in the sun while sipping on piña coladas usually prefer destinations where their raucous activities can be catered to. Those North Americans who go out of their way to find Álamos have most likely heard about it by word of mouth from another who has visited and found the town so charming they felt compelled to share it. They will eagerly tell you about the warmth of the townspeople, the beauty of the Spanish colonial architectural features, the feel of the cobblestones through the soles of their shoes, the smell of the Sonoran desert in the early morning, and the wispy fingers of clouds gently caressing the peaks of Mount Álamos and the surrounding Sierra Madre foothills. All the senses are stimulated to create the "feeling" that is Álamos, which once experienced, is not forgotten.

One gets a sense of the reverence with which Álamos is held, and the importance of the town in Sonora's history when first crossing the Arizona-Sonora border. *¿A donde vas?* is the routine question asked of each traveler presenting his or her documentation for immigrations approval at the Kilometer 21 stop just south of

Nogales. The simple, quiet answer of "Álamos" will usually be cause for a brief respectful pause, followed by *"Ah, Álamos. Tengo parientes de Álamos"*. Everyone who can is proud to mention they are direct descendants of, or closely related to someone from Álamos. Many Mexicans of Spanish descent make a pilgrimage to Álamos to visit the place of birth of an ancestor or relative. They will tour the church, museum, cemetery, and then walk the streets with the quiet veneration and respectfulness owed to hallowed ground.

Of course, the town is not for everyone. Sometimes after a cursory stroll around Álamos, a tourist may ask; "But, what is there to DO here?"

To which we always answer; "Well, there's nothing to do here. But it takes all day to do it!"

With the best of intentions, a quick run to the market for an innocent liter of milk can keep you away from home for hours, depending on who you bump into to chat with along the way, and where you go from there. And that is why I purposely have not left home this morning. I have decided to spend today in the kitchen, preparing enchaladas and flan for guests who will be joining us for dinner. I'm fully prepared, though, for interruptions. My hands are always into something, it seems, when there is another toc-toc-toc on the wrought-iron entry gate. Door-to-door vendors still frequent the neighborhoods, delivering bottled water, soliciting donations, or offering goods and services not likely to be available in any of the shops in the market area. It all adds to what is the *sabor* – flavor – of life here in Álamos.

My first unexpected visitor this morning is Roberto Grajeda Gastelum, or 'Shoeshine Bobby' as some of the North Americans call him. Bobby lives in *Barrio de Guayparines,* which abuts the dry arroyo running through the center of town. He is known all over Álamos for two things – his shoe shines and his beautiful, deep singing voice. Bobby's open air curbside enterprise near the market fits his lifestyle very well. With no overhead, no shingle, and no regular hours to keep, he can work when he wants and enjoy life to it's fullest. He may, from time to time, enjoy it so much that he is noticeably absent from his business locale, a rickety old wooden chair chained to a large, venerable cottonwood tree along the west side of the Alameda. A few days or a week later he'll return, a bit disheveled, perhaps, but with a smile on his face and ready to work again.

With the increasing popularity over the years of suede and man-made leather dress shoes, and synthetic and fabric athletic and everyday footwear, Bobby's walk-up business is sometimes slow. On those days, he may strike out with the tools of his trade in a plastic bag slung over his shoulder, going door-to-door in search of scuffed leather shoes or dusty boots needing a good wax and buff job. It is just such a day that brings him to our house. Bobby enjoys practicing his English, and is quick with a joke or a funny twist on words. After our greeting, I go to the bedroom closet, scrounge around for two or three pair of shoes, and bring them out to the front stoop for Bobby to shine. He moves to the shade of the *limón* tree and, humming a tune, gets to work. I go back to the kitchen.

In the Mexican culture, it seems that quite often visitations from friends and family are unexpected, drop-in occurrences. Everything stops, and the visitor will most certainly be invited in, staying until the host initiates that the time has arrived for departure. The fact that one may not be expecting, or have time for company does not enter into the mind of the caller. And so it will be today. It comes with a story of a special friendship.

The municipality of Álamos stretches many kilometers to the north and south of the actual town itself. Many small *ejidos* (government-granted ranching communes) dot the county-sized territory. *Ejido* residents struggle to make ends meet by ranching or growing crops of corn, beans, squash, sorghum, or sesame seed. They harvest and sell whatever produce and seed that their livestock or the birds don't eat first. Migratory white-wing and mourning doves love to feast on the seed crops. There is a generous government-controlled hunting season for these birds extending from November through to March, attracting sportsmen from the United States and Canada to visit this region during the winter months. Their experiences are enhanced by the services of professional organizers who provide customized packages including room, board, licenses, ammunition, and retrieval services of downed birds by *ejido* resident 'bird-boys'.

My husband and our labrador, Gina, have enjoyed dozens of dove hunts in the fields south of Álamos, and Bill and I have become acquainted with some of the people who live in the *ejido* he most often frequents. "Chapo", grandly named Gildardo Armando León Juárez, has been shagging birds for Bill for about fifteen years. Over time, Bill and I have met Chapo's family, and have become good friends. Though their home is rustic and their lifestyle simple, they always welcome us with open arms and will share anything they may have. We have done likewise, usually giving them the downed birds from each hunt, bringing them gifts at Christmas, and contributing toward celebrations of birthdays and other special events. So when any of the family members come into town, they will go out of their way to stop by our home for a visit. Few families own their own vehicle, so a trip into Álamos for someone who lives out on an *ejido* involves getting a ride on any vehicle heading to town. This could be hitching a ride in the open back of a friend or relative's truck, or using the local bus that provides once-daily service to many outlying ranchos. Bus fare is twenty pesos each way, so a trip to town must have purpose before it is undertaken.

So I simply cannot ignore the persistent knocking and calling that now starts at the front door. It is Chapo's sister and other family members who have accompanied her elderly, widowed mother of the family on the bus from Gerocoa to pick up her monthly social security allotment. Recipients must appear in person at the Social Security clinic on *Calle Rosales* on the appointed day, with their government-issued retirement credential card in hand to receive the monthly cash sum amounting to about one thousand pesos. This amount is used by the recipient to cover the purchase of personal, household, and discretionary items until the next apportion the following month. Chapo's mother is the matriarch of her family. Other than their communal share of crop sales in the fall, cattle sales, and bird-boy services provided by some of the *ejido* men, there is no other income. You can imagine what a stretch it is for the family to make ends meet.

I invite my unexpected visitors in from the street to our inner courtyard seating, and offer them a soda and some cookies. Our conversation runs the gamut of the weather and their health as well as recent activities in and about town. Finally, I get up from my chair and tell my guests that it is time for me to return to the kitchen, and they remind me on their way out of the upcoming birthday celebration to be held out on their ranch this coming

Saturday, wanting to verify that we will, indeed, be attending. I assure them wholeheartedly, and after *abrazos y besos* they depart.

Back in the kitchen, I have just enough time to temper the scalded milk and heavy cream mixture into the whisked egg yolks and sugar in preparation for this evening's flan, when there is another rap at the door. The rhythmic metallic sound on the gate I immediately recognize as belonging to the 'tamale lady', Albina Quijada Palomares, and the time of day indicates that she is making her way home from selling lunch time tamales around the *Palacio*, our town's City Hall building. She is a rotund, middle-aged little lady with pudgy Santa Claus cheeks and a smile to match. Her beef, bean, and sweet-corn tamales are freshly made by her own hands each morning, as generously sized as she is, and truly some of the best I've ever eaten. The tamales cost five pesos each, and are a filling lunch or dinner entre.

Albina's visits started a couple of years ago, when one hot day she arrived at the door red-faced and out of breath, asking if she might have a glass of water. I invited her into the shade of our inner courtyard to rest and refresh herself, starting a ritual that we have continued once a week or so ever since. She always comes in and sits a spell as we talk, discussing our families, her hardships (as the mother of two and wife of an invalid, diabetic husband), and life in general. At the end of our conversation for that day, she'll slip the last few of the plump, warm, beef tamales she has been saving for me into a plastic bag, and tie the top into that curiously secure little knot that only Mexicans know how to make, and set them on the table.

I pay her and get up to indicate my return to the kitchen, and Albina also rises in preparation for the remainder of her walk home. Both kettles which earlier in the day contained dozens of tamales are now empty, but her little black zipper coin-purse bulges with pesos which will be judiciously apportioned to purchase more tamale-making supplies, pay toward her children's education, and keep the household solvent. Tomorrow she will get up *con el favor de Dios* and do it all again.

It is after this visit with Albina that Lupe, who has stayed just within ear reach in the background, divulges to me that she used to send her son, Jorge, out to sell tamales too. Lupe said she made them and Jorge went out when he was seven or eight years old and peddle them door-to-door. She quickly added that hers were really good, and that they always sold fast. It is hard to imagine the Jorge Garcia that Bill and I now know – U.S. citizen, happily married father of two, and a successful jet and turbine engine aircraft mechanic – was at one time selling tamales on the streets of Álamos, but so it was almost thirty years ago.

When I make this comment to Bill, he muses, "It's a curious phenomenon that people born and raised in Álamos always feel that need to come back. The town stays alive in their hearts as a small burning flame that flares up from time to time demanding to be nourished and fed by a return visit. If you are born in Álamos, you can never really ever leave Álamos"

Perhaps this helps to explain why Jorge relishes his infrequent return visits to the place of his birth; and the place of a Mexican's birth is celebrated as much or more than any other achievement in their life.

It is mid-afternoon, and my dinner preparations are almost complete. I am neither surprised nor annoyed to hear yet another tapping on the gate outside our door. This time, I do not recognize the young lady standing at the entryway; but she identifies herself as an official census taker, and shows her credentials. Clipboard in hand, she is canvassing the neighborhood and wants to ask a few questions that she insists will only take a few minutes of my time, so I oblige and invite her into the *sala*.

At first, the questions are routine demographic and statistical inquiries which she rattles off, and I answer readily. How many people live in this household? Do we rent or own this dwelling? What educational level did you and your spouse achieve? What are your occupations? And so on....

Then, she asks a couple of interesting domestic questions. First, she wants to know if we cook with wood or gas. Electricity is not even an option. I answer that we cook with gas. Her next question is even more curious:

"Do you sleep in your kitchen?"

"No, we do not!", I answer with a slight chuckle under my breath.

After a few final questions, the young girl thanks me for our participation in the poll and places a large sticker on the front door on her way out to indicate that our household had taken part in the census. We say *adiós*, and as she moves on to the neighbor's house, I lean against the open doorway to ponder the "sleeping in the kitchen" question.

It turns out that this one question can determine the economic viability of a municipality in Mexico. A family living in a basic one-room house will perform all of their daily activities in that one room, including food preparation and cooking, and then at night push things aside to make room for their Sonoran cots or beds in order to sleep. The next morning, bedding will be rolled up or moved aside so that daily activities can once again take place. A family who "sleeps" in their kitchen most likely will have a one-room house; whereas a family who does not sleep in their kitchen most likely will have at least one additional room that might be used as a bedroom. Based on knowing how many households sleep in their kitchens -vs- those who do not, a governing agency can quickly surmise the level of financial achievement for that population. This is important and necessary data for an administration trying to determine prosperity, or lack thereof of any community. What better question to ask?

A glance at the sky tells me that our usually pleasant weather seems to be deteriorating. Gathering clouds have already obscured the highest peaks of the mountains to the west. Lupe had told me this morning, under perfectly blue, sunny skies, that rain was in the forecast. Without the benefit of radio, television, or computer, her predictions are proving to be correct.

Before nightfall, I cover our supply of firewood out back. A winter rain means chilly temperatures; and with guests coming a warm fire in our *chimenea* (fireplace) will really feel good.

Solemnly, the father positions the two boys directly in front of the tiny altar before directing them to make a proper sign of the cross.

CHAPTER 6

Friday

Bill and I waken to the sound of rain falling on the skylights and water spouting from the roof-top *canales*. It has been raining since midnight, and doesn't appear to be letting up anytime soon.

We tiptoe from our bedroom barefoot across the interior patio puddled with cold rainwater, to the kitchen to light a fire, make coffee and start the day. Our small kitchen and *sala* always are a snug and cozy asylum in cool or rainy weather. This section of our house dates back to the 1750's, and the meter-thick adobe walls help to keep interior temperatures constant, regardless of outside fluctuations. Lupe had thoughtfully prepared both of the *chimeneas* for lighting prior to her departure yesterday, and soon the glowing flames are licking the dry mesquite wood creating a warmth and friendliness that only a real fire can give. There is no such thing as central heating or cooling of homes here. Fireplaces here in Álamos are a relatively recent restoration feature; added for focal points and practical use during the revival of the colonial central part of town over the past fifty years.

Weather in this region of Mexico is an interesting phenomenon. A unique dry, tropical deciduous forest region, Álamos receives the majority of it's twenty-six inches (660 millimeters) of annual rainfall during the summer monsoon – a period of six to eight weeks from July to September. Monsoon rains are depended upon to raise the water table, fill wells, replenish reservoirs, and water crops. Locals will tell you that the traditional date for the gathering clouds over the Sierra Madre to deliver the first summer showers used to be the *Día de San Juan*, Day of Saint John, the 24th of June. But the rains have been starting later and later – at times well into July – and Lupe, a devout Catholic, tells me that is because the people have lost their faith. They no longer believe, and it was the like-mindedness of the belief that brought the rains every year at the same time. The faith that can move mountains no longer exists here, Lupe says. And that is why the monsoonal weather patterns have changed, crops do not always receive the timely rains they need to develop and grow, and water has become scarce.

In contrast to the summer monsoon winter precipitation is unpredictable and scant. The area remains dry unless a Pacific low pressure system dips down from the western United States, or a late-season hurricane blows in from the southern Baja region. Whenever that happens, the resulting rains that fall in and around Álamos are welcome because they serve to rinse down the streets, settle the dusty air, and provide moisture for plantings and greenery, transforming a grey, dormant, landscape almost overnight to lively shades of green.

Rainy days are an understood day off for our house keeper. It is not possible to sweep the patio, tend the garden, or do any real cleaning, and more than likely, Lupe is busy at home looking after leaky roofs and collecting rain water for later use. All over town things are quiet, with little or no pedestrian or vehicular traffic. As the morning progresses, I can get a feeling for the slackening intensity of the rainfall by listening to the *canales* out over the patio. The cascading streams of water slow to a dribble, and then stop as the skies slowly start to open, revealing hints of jewel-like blueness. The rain has moved eastward to blanket the higher elevations of the Sierra Madre, and slowly the town begins to stir once again.

People start to come out from their sanctums of refuge from the rain, some on errands and others, like me, want to get out of the house just to stretch "cabin legs" after having been inside most of the morning. I head out on foot toward the *Mirador*, an elevated vantage point, located up on what used to be called *perico* hill, on the southern end of town. There seems to be a lot of congestion at the *arroyo* crossing going out on the *Camino Real* road. The usually-dry *arroyo* is running water at about eight to ten inches at the deepest part. Vehicular traffic is reduced to single-file for crossing the flowing waters. Some of the lower-slung cars have crossed too eagerly, and now are parked where their engines sputtered and gave out, with their hoods up, drying out. Trucks can pass with little or no problem. We pedestrians use the old but well constructed elevated foot bridge to cross and keep our feet dry. The congestion, confusion, and crossing provide quite the diversion and entertainment for the rubber-necking on-lookers. A few people are standing idly by watching to see which of the approaching vehicles dare to try crossing, and which will turn around to go elsewhere. Small children are scampering around, picking up loose, floatable refuse that missed being swept away by the rushing current, and tossing it into the water to watch the velocity at which it will be carried downstream.

Leaving the excitement behind, I continue my walk up to the *Mirador*. Turning off the southbound *Camino Real* the steep, damp and slippery, cobbled path rises for three hundred feet, ending at a well-groomed area on top which provides an overall view of the town reawakening from the morning showers.

Mount Álamos still remains shrouded by clouds, but the blue patches of opening sky directly overhead indicate that conditions are clearing rapidly. From the high vantage point the *Mirador* provides, I can see the normally dry washes running on all sides. This runoff will flow south, some seeping into the ground-water table, and the excess eventually reaching the reservoirs near El Fuerte in Sinaloa, the neighboring state just a few miles to the south. The breeze here on the *Mirador* is cool and refreshing, and the air smells of wet mesquite, palo verde, and musky damp earth.

I pick my way back down the cobblestone path and return to the center of town by a slightly different route, following *Calle Chihuahua*, along which there is a colorful, yet reverent sidewalk shrine to the Virgin of Guadalupe. It is set into an adobe wall and protected by ornamental wrought-iron, with fresh flowers and burning candles adorning the beautiful tile-mural painting of the Virgin contained within. Dozens of these religious icons are scattered all over town. Many Mexicans who pass them will stop briefly or make a gesture to cross themselves as they proceed, in subtle recognition of their Catholic faith and beliefs. As I approach, a father with two young boys stops to look in at the Virgin. Solemnly, the father positions the boys directly in front of the tiny altar and directs them to make a proper sign of the cross before they continue on their way. This is how traditions are passed on: from father to son. Will these young boys grow up and carry on that same tradition with their sons?

A nice looking dog befriends me about half way down *Calle Galeana*. She's a cute, caramel-colored girl with distinctive white markings on her paws, neck, and the very tip of her tail. Obviously well fed, but wearing no collar or identification, she prances a few steps in front of me and then stops, turns, and waits for me to catch up. I have a few doggie treats in my fanny-pack, so I offer her one; and then another, and continue on my way. The pup decides to follow me, and so we walk on like old friends, silent, yet in each other's presence, all the way out to the soccer field, on the busy road at the entry to Álamos. I decide to jog one lap around the field, so I do, accompanied by my new companion, who keeps just ahead of my pace, all the while looking back for assurance that I am still there. She doesn't seem to be very cautious or wary about being so far from her home territory, whichever *barrio* that is, and seems to have no fear of the traffic now starting to pick up after the rain.

Heading back into central Álamos, I caution my new-found friend about the dangers of being out in the road amidst the traffic (as if she can understand English!?!!) when my worst fears are realized. In trying to avoid one outbound vehicle, she runs right into the path of an in-bound car and is hit – hard.

The dog tumbles and rolls and yelps, and I freeze in horror and scream. The errant driver never stops for even a moment, but continues on into town. Somehow, the animal rights herself, but is wailing and crying and tears-off running liked a crazed savage down the road back through the traffic and into town, yelping all the way. I quickly lose sight of her, so there is not even a chance to follow and check her condition. Is she OK? Or does pure adrenalin allow her just enough energy to run off some place to lick her wounds; or worse yet, to succumb to internal injuries and die? I will never really know, yet I think I do know, as she doesn't reappear on my future walks around Álamos.

It is difficult to shake off what I have just witnessed, but I slowly walk on, drying my tears and composing myself before reaching the *Mercado* on the *Alameda* for a bit of shopping before returning home. Everyone appears happy for the recent rains, but the shopkeepers are most grateful that the precipitation has stopped so that they can conduct business again. In an attempt to keep floors clean and dry inside shopkeepers place cut and flattened cardboard boxes at the entryway to most stores to catch moisture off patrons' shoes. Street vendors can finally open their stands to sell tacos, bean soup, hot-dogs and *sopa de mariscos* to passers-by. I make my purchases in the *Mercado* of fresh salad vegetables, broccoli, a mild Chihuahua cheese, and some milk. The last part of my long walk takes me from the market area up the *callejón de beso* to the more tranquil church plaza, which I cut across on my way home.

Where has this day gone? It is already late afternoon, and Bill and I try to reserve this special time of day for an activity we have learned from our Mexican friends -- the custom of sitting outside on the porch or stoop to simply chat and be in the moment of watching Álamos say good bye to the daylight and slip into darkness. The ritual starts with carrying two plastic chairs and a small *equipale* table outside our front door to the elevated porch area. Pouring two glasses of wine and inviting our black labrador to come out with us, we take our places. Not missing a beat, we will sip our wine, discuss the day's events, and interject a friendly *Adiós,* the all-inclusive "hello-goodbye", to passers-by. From our vantage point, we can see not only busy *Calle Comercio*, but also skyward towards the *Mirador*; still bathed in the last light of day. Those who have gathered up there enjoy the fleeting rays of the sun as it settles behind the hills. Two home-made kites bobble on the invisible winds.

Darkness arrives, and the city street lights illuminate the way for evening pedestrians, making it easier for them to navigate our cobblestone street. Bill and I stay outside nursing the last of our wine, and watch as the light of the evening planets and stars intensifies, then bring chairs, table, and dog inside, have dinner, and head to bed for a good nights rest. In turning off the living room lights, I casually observe and ignore a two-inch spider on the wall at about eye-level. He belongs here in this *casa* more than I probably do, so I pay him the respect of letting him live. He and I will most likely be here tomorrow, and hopefully the next day, and beyond as guardians of these thick adobe walls we both call our home.

"Spiderman" is quickly dismembered, and "Tigger" is full of candy and oranges.

Chapter 7

Saturday

We are happy that Saturday dawns clear, sunny, and warm. Today is the day of little Guillermo's birthday party at Chapo's village of Gerocoa, and as promised, Bill and I plan to attend.

Birthdays, baptisms, first communions, weddings, anniversaries and holidays are all celebrated by Mexicans enthusiastically, with only the size of a family's pocketbook dictating the amount or quality of food, drink, entertainment or decor. The location of the gathering can be a simple backyard, or a rented grand *salón*, but the excitement level stays the same.

Mexican etiquette dictates that we take our cue from the time indicated when invited to a party and arrive a few hours later. So, when Guillermo's family told us the party would be starting at 12:00 noon, we knew we could sleep in, eat a late breakfast, and get ready to leave the house a little before one-thirty.

Arrangements for this gathering started a few weeks earlier, when we gave Guillermo's family enough money to purchase a young pig that would be fattened, slaughtered and slow-cooked, *barbacoa*-style, with orange juice, prunes and spices as the main course. In addition, we have bought *piñatas*, (paper maché figures) a huge sheet cake, beer, soda, candy, presents, *albóndigas* (meat balls) and a platter of *camarónes* to take with us today on the 27 kilometer drive south of town to the small village of Gerocoa.

It is hard to imagine the rock-strewn, bumpy, well rutted road we are driving on as part of the original navigable *Camino Real* constructed as the communications lifeline between silver-rich Álamos and Mexico City over two hundred years ago. Following the terrain, we pick our way past the *Los Frailes* mountains, over the gently flowing *Mentidero* stream, further yet, finally turning east at a spot marked with white painted rocks and an old *Tecate* beer sign. Although Gerocoa is far removed from Álamos, it does have one thriving business located there – a beer *expendio* (retail sales location).

We have always thought that this little *rancho* community consisted of about three or four homes, in addition to the Tecate store, so today we expect to see maybe a few more children than those normally around when we drop off Chapo from a morning hunt. So it is quite a suprise when a throng of about thirty-five kids runs out to our truck as we pull up. The party word has spread to Las Flores, another small settlement nearby, and they have all turned out for the activities and fun Shortly after we unload our contributions and make the rounds shaking hands and greeting the adults, the first of three *piñatas*, a red, blue and black ruffled crepe-paper "Spiderman" is hung and ready to face his demise at the hands of the youngsters. The action figure character is quickly dismembered with well placed blows, and replaced by a curious large six-sided see-through box structure filled with colorful balloons and covered with cellophane. This pinata proves tougher than it looks, and even some of the adults are tempted to take a whack at it. The operator at the other end of the rope has done this before, and is a deft manipulator.

When the cube finally succumbs to the blows and breaks apart, the balloons create yet another diversion as they must all be chased down and popped. The final pinata is a life-sized, smiling "Tigger", full of candy and oranges. He dances at the end of his halter for quite some time, losing body parts but refusing to break open. An eight-year-old winds up and swings, striking a weak spot. The gash opens "Tigger" up and he spills his guts, much to the delight of all of the small children waiting with anticipation. Amid screams of joy and excitement, they scamper like *mochomos* (ants) to retrieve the scattered sweet contents. One very small boy, still in diapers, is left empty-handed. Probably new to the pinata routine, he wasn't big enough or quick enough to muscle his way in. The other children are already gone, and the ground is as clean as a whistle. He plops down right there and starts to cry, big oversized alligator tears running down his dusty little cheeks. Mom has a word with an older sister, the little one is given a share of his sibling's take, and everyone is happy again.

Someone turns on a portable boom-box, and *ranchero* music fills the air. Attention now turns to the long table bearing Guillermo's presents, a sheet-cake, two-liter bottles of soda, a big glass container of the corn starch based drink *horchata*, plastic cups, and a smaller cake. The youngsters are given a piece of the dessert and a drink while parents and relatives sit around on chairs to watch and chat.

The huge covered washtub containing the well seasoned *barbacoa* that has been slow-cooked for hours in an open pit is now simmering over an outdoor campfire, fork-tender, and ready to be served. Nearby, pots of refried beans, potatoes and carrots await on the elevated adobe-brick outdoor cooking area. Hot corn tortillas complete the menu. This is the typical Sonoran celebration meal; and as it is dished up to the grownups, we pass the meatballs and shrimp as an added garnish. The children are much more interested in their cake, soda pop and running around than eating dinner. Dogs pick up anything dropped, snatching a bite or two off any plate set down within their reach. (I lose half of my cake this way.) Chickens scratch and peck at the crumbs. Everyone eats their fill.

After eating, I sit for awhile with some of the children, making balloon figures for curious eyes. Bill conducts a *lotteria* (raffle) with the younger kids to give away a large soft stuffed doll and a sturdy plastic dump-truck to the lucky winners. The shy girl with the long black braids has number 18, and is given the doll, and the boy with number 11 is awarded the truck. Meanwhile, the smaller cake and the presents have quietly been removed from the children's table to the interior of the two-room dirt-floor house to be opened and enjoyed by immediate family members the next day, as is the custom.

The party is still going strong by the time we are ready to leave. Almost one hundred adults and children are enjoying the celebration, and it shows no signs of breaking up soon. Bill sends someone over to the *expendio de Tecate* with pesos to buy more cold beer so the festivities can continue. We circulate among all the adults to shake their hands, hug and kiss, and say good-bye before getting in the truck for the bumpy drive back to Álamos. We have enjoyed sharing this particular moment with Chapo and his family. Few of the American residents here have the chance to experience what we did today – an invitation to share in a Mexican traditional celebration in it's simplest, most basic form. The forty-minute ride back into town gives us the chance to reflect on how lucky we are to have such good friends among the people of this area.

Not every celebration is this rudimentary. The variations on the party theme run the gamut and the decibel level from medium to deafening. If the hosts can afford a live band for their event, the quality and resonance of the music can produce a beat that will be felt to the marrow of the bones, and will be heard across many barrios. Everyone dances. Even the horses dance. The *charrería* culture is another thread in the fabric which envelops the Mexican spirit, introduced when *Conquistadores* with their horses arrived on this continent. It includes the sport of dancing horses and has survived to this century.

One incident that happened as a result of this passion for music and dance is neither enjoyable to write about, nor read; but it is a story that must be told. Lupe's brother, Ramón "Pablo" Macias, and his horse, *Azabache* (whose name means 'black in color') attended a party celebrating a baptism about a year ago. The little one in whose honor the event was being held was long asleep in his bed, as the music played on and on.

A horse and rider who have been together for many years form a bond, and can move as one. Imperceptible movements of the *caballero* in his saddle command and control starts, turns stops, and hoof movements of the huge animal beneath him. With time, the horse can read the mind of his master, and a good rider can actually coax his horse to prance his hooves to the beat of any music being played. The horse will dance as long as the rider wants, to the point of building up a sweat and frothing. Despite the strenuous rigors of training to dance, Azabache remained a gentle steed, who even allowed the most timid to mount and ride him.

Sometimes other horses and their riders join in, and a competitive mentality overrides all reason. Onlookers watch, drink beer, and nod approvingly as the huge steeds perform their frisky shuffle. And so it was on this particular night. The music played, and Pablo and Azabache "danced" their duet, totally unaware that their dance floor actually was the protective cover over the host family's in-ground water storage system. The pounding hooves accelerated the degradation of the unreinforced cover to the point that it gave way, and both horse and rider fell six to seven meters into the water-filled *pozo*.

Amid shrieks and screams from both, Pablo was quickly pulled out, but a *grua* (tow) truck had to be called to winch out the much heavier, drowning horse, who suffered multiple broken bones in the fall. The horse had buffered Pablo's descent sufficiently so that he had no serious injuries, but as a precaution, he was taken immediately to the hospital and kept overnight for observation. Azabache was finally pulled from the depths, but had to be put down due to his injuries. The horse had broken Pablo's fall, and had allowed him to walk away virtually injury free, except for the huge hole in his heart that resulted as a loss of his best companion.

Pablo was told of the horse's death while in the hospital and immediately insisted that a back-hoe be hired to dig a hole on his property large enough to bury Azabache. This request went entirely in the face of "custom". Ordinarily, the horse would have been processed quickly as a source of meat for human consumption. Pablo honored his best friend by sparing him the humiliation and degradation of being used for sustenance, and now grieves at the loss each time he passes the burial mound on his property. He may never again have such a talented, devoted animal in his possession. The *charrería* traditions of Mexico, which include the dancing of horses, are still a vital part of life here, and must be respected for that reason.

Returning from our afternoon out in the country and entering our house with all it's conveniences and creature-comforts makes us feel rather self-indulgent and gives us pause for reflection. All these items are just things, none of which are truly necessary for a full and satisfying life. Today we experienced the real formula for happiness – the love and appreciation of family and friends and the enjoyment of each moment as it arrives.

Still full from our late lunch out at Gerocoa, Bill and I decide to skip having a big dinner, and instead walk over to the place where we first fell in love with each other – and with Álamos – the *Casa de los Tesoros* (House of Treasures) Hotel. Located on Calle Obregón, just one street over from our house, it's where we stayed on our early visits to Álamos twenty-five years go. It was also in the courtyard of the Tesoros Hotel where our wedding ceremony took place on the afternoon of December 31st, 1986.

Although ownership has changed over the past quarter century, a few of the employees we met all those many years ago at "The Tesoros" still work there, so it is like coming home to be greeted by name as we take a seat in their cozy front bar area close to the blazing corner *chimenea* for a drink and a snack. The trio of guitarists that has played there each evening for as long as anyone can remember – Rosario Alcantar, Rodolfo Hurtado, and Gabriel Hurtado– starts playing what has become "our song", *Dos Arbolitos*, a *caballero's* ballad of his loneliness out in the campo, and of the two small entwined trees that remind him of the love he can only hope for. We never tire of hearing the song, so listen intently to the trio as we are served the *Casa's* signature margarita, prepared by Jose Luis, and a snack of chips and salsa. After a few more songs, another round of margaritas, and friendly conversation with everyone in the bar, we say good-night to all and stroll hand in hand down Calle Obregón toward home humming *"Dos Arbolitos"* under the watchful eye of the full moon and the constellation Orion.

Dos Arbolitos

Han nacido en mi rancho dos arbolitos,
Dos arbolitos que parecen gemelos;
Y desde mi casita los veo solitos
Bajo el amparo santo y la luz del cielo.
Nunca estan separados uno del otro,
Porque asi quiso Dios que los dos nacieran;
Y con sus mismas ramas se hacen caricias
Como si fueran novios que se quisieran.

Arbolito, arbolito, bajo tu sombra
Voy a esperar que el dia cansado muera;
Y cuando estoy solito mirando al cielo
Pido pa' que me mande una compañera.

Cuando estoy a mis sembras y a los maizales,
Entre los surcos riego todo mi llanto;
Solo tengo de amigos mis animales
A los que con tristeza siempre les canto.
Las vacas, los novillos y los becerros
Saben que necesito que alguien me quiera;
Y mi caballo pinto y hasta mi perro
Han cambiando y me miran de otra manera.

Arbolito, arbolito, me siento solo;
Quiero que me acompañes hasta que muera.

EPILOGUE

On the evening of October 11th 2008, Hurricane Norbert blew in from the Gulf of California, over the beach town of Huatabampito and inland toward Álamos. The area already was saturated from prolific summer rains and the terrain simply could not hold any additional moisture. The resulting precipitation caused a series of huge mud-slides that originated in the higher elevations of Mount Álamos and headed directly for the town of Álamos, tearing up and carrying along everything in its path. A seven-foot wall of ravaging sludge, mud, muck, cars, trees, boulders, homes, and even human beings, surged through the town's lower lying arroyos and the municipal market area. In twenty terrifying minutes under cover of night, the entire landscape of the town was changed. Everything in the way had been picked up and deposited further down stream. Over fifty homes were totally destroyed and two hundred others were severely damaged with contents lost. All businesses in the Alameda and Mercado were washed out with the contents damaged beyond recovery. Roads and bridges were swept away, severing one side of the town from the other, and from the outside world. Electricity and telephone land line service was cut off, and water and sewer lines were uprooted. With the arrival of the first rays of light on the morning of the 12th of October, a totally different landscape greeted the people of Álamos. Everyone was grateful just to be alive, and incredible stories of luck, life, and survival were being told everywhere.

News of the disaster quickly spread. Clean-up, and rebuilding began immediately. Sonoran television reports and personal videos started circulating via the news and internet for the world to see. Even before the initial period of shock, sadness, and mourning had passed, help arrived. Mexican government agencies moved in heavy equipment and medical aid, and within hours, power was restored. With the cutting of international red tape, a monumental airlift effort initiated by the Baja Bush Pilots organization brought over forty aircraft <u>directly</u> to Álamos from the U.S. with food, water, clothing, and tools. Shelters were established around town, and every hotel or restaurant with functioning kitchen facilities kept working around the clock to provide meals. Thousands of truck loads of debris and dirt were cleared out of the way and deposited south of town, so homes, shops and streets could be cleaned and disinfected.

As quickly as only thirteen days after the innundation, the first of the market area businesses reopened. The North Americans who were here worked to exhaustion side-by-side with the native Alamensens in a display of true solidarity in the face of such adversity. Many North American friends of Álamos who were not here donated monetarily toward the recovery. Although there are permanent visual, economic and emotional scars that never will completely heal, all who have contributed and worked so hard are pleased and proud of the restored, revived Álamos emerging from the mud and dirt. The casual visitor or tourist may think that the town has recovered, and in the superficial, cosmetic sense the more visible areas look that way. But the deep scars of shock, fear, and monumental loss are branded on the hearts of all who witnessed the event, and those scars remain to temper the future. The work continues, and will continue for a long time to come.

Typical of the Mexican spirit, though, is the thread of optimism that is woven into their backbone.

And so there are changes. *Barrio Guayparines*, where "Shoeshine Bobby" lives, was one of the residential areas hardest hit by Hurricane Norbert because of its low proximity to the *Arroyo de Aduana*. Bobby recalls vividly that terrible night when he had to cling to an overhanging timber while holding a small child in his arms waiting for the flash flooding to subside. They both survived, but he lost his home and all of his possessions. But with a smile on his face Bobby will tell you about his new red shoe-shine chair on the Alameda – a gift from the City of Álamos. The old one had been beat up beyond repair by the surging waters. He is grateful for his life, and prepared to carry on.

For the time being, Sunday shoppers must look for their favorite *tianguis* vendors either on the raised Alameda near the city market shopping area, or out on the soccer-field at the entry to town. The area around the arroyo is undergoing a major facelift with heavy equipment and earth movers repositioning channels for future water run-off, and trenching for an improved sewer and water treatment system.

Don Martín Leyva, the elderly gentleman I met in front of his house on Calle Galleana, has returned to his home after spending a trial period in a nursing home facility in Álamos. The religious order of sisters who care for the residents frowned on the slightest consumption of alcohol on the property, so Martín decided to return home. He is still being looked in on by helpful neighbors.

Descendants of native Alamensens and Mexican and American tourists still visit Álamos. The airstrip north of town has been lengthened, securely fenced, is well guarded, and most recently has been designated to become an international airport offering all associated services to non-commercial aircraft arriving from the United States; including customs, immigration, and flight service operations.

Albina is still making and selling tamales door to door with a slight inflationary price increase of one peso to six pesos each. Her daughter has completed her education, is fluent in written and spoken English, and is an accomplished artist working in multiple mediums.

Lupe, our attentive and faithful housekeeper still works with us on a daily basis. She is a spry sixty-something grandmother of six, who brings a smile to work every day, and continues to share all her family and neighborhood happenings with me as she sweeps the patio. She is approaching retirement age; but assures us she would rather die with a broom in her hands rather than give up work and sit around with less to do. We love her dearly.

There will be another census here next year (2010). Will the questions be the same? Or will other questions be crucial to determining the economic viability of this and other communities ten years after the last accounting?

Dogs still wander the streets. A determined effort has been made by some private enterprises to spay or neuter and find homes for stray and abandoned animals, and this appears to be helping. Last week, our houseguest and I took an early morning walk up to the Mirador. About halfway along our route a sweet, caramel-colored female pup with distinctive white markings on her paws, neck, and the very tip of her tail met up with us, and accompanied us all of the way to the Mirador look-out, and back down to Calle Comercio. She walked with a slight limp, as if compensating for an injury received some time ago that may not have completely healed. I would love to think that my canine friend from the soccer field had found me once again.

Celebrations of life and death are still the nuclear binding force that drives the community. Baptisms, *Quinces*, weddings, and funerals continue to be the traditional, established occasions that allow young and old to breathe the same air of their culture.

We still relish the opportunity to sit out on our porch in the evenings and greet passers-by with a friendly "*Adiós*."

Spiders still drop in for a visit at our *casa* from time to time. We continue to give each other space, as silent acknowledgment of each others contribution as caretakers of these thick adobe walls we temporarily call our home.

Pablo Macias sold a piece of his ranch property to purchase a new young horse, *El Dorado* (shiny one), and they are learning to move together as one element to the distinctive beat of Mexican music.

The spirit of Álamos is imbedded deep in our hearts and our minds, and pulls at us each time we get removed from it's invisible, magnetic embrace. It is my hope that you have come to understand why this small Sonoran town endears itself to all who visit. May your travels bring you here someday to walk over these cobblestones, or perhaps bring you back again to experience the "feeling" that is Álamos.

ACKNOWLEDGMENTS

I thank my best friend and husband, Bill, for introducing me to Álamos over a quarter-century ago. I must also thank that casual stranger who told Bill about Álamos, over a drink at a bar in Bisbee, Arizona, some years before that.

Many thanks to those who kindly reviewed my story prior to its publication: Jo Ann Ridley, Donna Love, Leila Gillette, Bev Krucek and Robert Cabot.

BOOKS AND WEBSITES

REFERRED TO AND

RECOMMENDED:

Alamada, Karina. Álamos - Pueblo Magico. Editorial Garabatos, Hermosillo, Mexico, 2006.

www.Álamosportfolio.com A presentation of Álamos business and residential community. Dan Veenstra, moderator.

www.yahoogroups.com/Álamosnews An electronic resource for current information about Álamos. Ron Granich, moderator.

Bowden, Charles. The Secret Forest. University of New Mexico Press, NM., 1993.

Castillo, Juan V. Álamos - Por los Siglos de los Siglos. Mexico. Editorial Garabatos, Hermosillo, Mexico. 2007

Corbala Acuna, Manuel S. Álamos de Sonora. Institute Sonorense de Cultura, Mexico, D.F., 1989.

Escalante, Guadalupe Macias. Interview and personal conversations. Álamos, Sonora, Mexico, 1987-2009.

Fitch, Robert L. Álamos, Mexico - The Way it Was. Coburg Printing, Eugene, OR., 1993.

Franklin, Ida Luisa. Ghosts of Álamos. Three Rivers Press, Denver, OR., 1980.

Franklin, Ida Luisa. Las Delicias. Three Rivers Press, Denver, CO., 1964.

French, Rachel. "Álamos - Sonora's City of Silver". The Smoke

Signal. Spring 1962, No.5. (reprint article), pp 1-16. Tucson, AZ. Spring, 1962.

Gillette, Lelia. The Stately Homes, of Álamos. Centro Graphico del Noroeste, S.A. de C.V., Mexico, 2006.

Gordon, Alvin J. Never Lose your Discouragements. Arcus Publishing Co., Sonoma, CA., 1989.

Gordon, Alvin J. and Gordon Darley. Álamos, Silver City of the Sierra Madre. 1955.

Hilton, John W. Sonora Sketch Book. The Macmillian Co.,New York, 1947.

Miles, Carlotta. Alamada of Álamos. Arizona Silouettes, Tucson, AZ., 1962.

Museo Costumbrista de Sonora. Álamos Sonora, Mexico. Information from visual displays.

Ridley, JoAnn. An Álamos Handbook. bk.d Productions, Álamos, Sonora, Mexico, 2004.

Stagg, Albert. The Alamadas and Álamos, 1783-1867. U of A Press, Tucson, AZ., 1976.

Urrea de Figueroa, Otalia. My Youth in Álamos. Dolisa Publications, Glendale, CA., 1983.

www.whatscookingamerica.net/pomelo.htm 10/10/2008.

Yetman, David. E-mail to the author. 2008

Yetman, David, and Van Devender, Thomas R. Mayo Ethnobotany. Berkley: University of California Press. 2002.

Printed in the United States
by Baker & Taylor Publisher Services